Charles Dickens

OLIVER TWIST

Kalyani Navyug Media Pvt Ltd
New Delhi

Charles Dickens

OLIVER TWIST

Sitting around the Campfire, telling the story, were:

WORDSMITH **DAN JOHNSON**

ILLUSTRATOR **RAJESH NAGULAKONDA**

COLOURIST **PRINCE VARGHESE**

LETTERER **GHAN SHYAM JOSHI**

EDITORS **EMAN CHOWDHARY & ADITI RAY**

EDITOR (INFORMATIVE CONTENT) **RASHMI MENON**

PRODUCTION CONTROLLER **VISHAL SHARMA**

ART DIRECTOR **RAJESH NAGULAKONDA**

COVER ART **ANIL C K**

DESIGN **JAYAKRISHNAN K P**

CAMPFIRE™

www.campfire.co.in

Published by Kalyani Navyug Media Pvt Ltd

101 C, Shiv House, Hari Nagar Ashram, New Delhi 110014 India

ISBN: 978-93-80028-10-1

ABOUT THE AUTHOR

Born in Portsmouth, England, on 7th February 1812, Charles John Huffam Dickens was one of eight children. His father, John, worked as a government clerk, but was imprisoned during Charles's childhood due to outstanding debts. This forced Charles to support his family by going to work in a boot-blacking factory at the age of twelve.

Although Dickens went on to receive a middle-class education at Wellington House Academy, he continued to work at the factory. His experiences of the different elements of society influenced many of the novels he would write later in life.

In 1827, Dickens left the Academy and began working as a law clerk, the first in a series of odd jobs. It wasn't until 1834 that he moved into the publishing world. His first job in this industry was as a reporter for the *Morning Chronicle*. Two years later, Dickens not only saw the first of his stories published, but also married Catherine Hogarth. By 1837, Dickens's stories had been collected into his first novel, *The Pickwick Papers*.

Dickens's novels initially appeared as serialised publications, a common practice at the time. It helped fuel his popularity with fans who eagerly anticipated each new installment of his stories. The plight of the poor became one of the major themes in Charles Dickens's novels – a reflection of the bitterness he felt about the way working-class people lived and were treated.

Considered to be one of England's greatest writers, some of Dickens's most famous works include *Oliver Twist*, *A Tale of Two Cities*, *David Copperfield*, and *A Christmas Carol*. Charles Dickens died on 9th June 1870.

In a certain town, among the other public buildings, stands a workhouse. Here, nine years ago, a young lad was born. He was named Oliver Twist.

Oliver's mother had been found in the street. No one ever knew much about her. She died as Oliver took his first breath of life.

After ten months at the main workhouse, Oliver was sent to a branch workhouse. There he stayed with other juvenile offenders whose only crime had been poverty. They lived there under their elderly matron, Mrs Mann.

The board made regular visits to the workhouse. They always made sure to send the parish beadle*, Mr Bumble, to the workhouse the day before they arrived. It was Mr Bumble's duty to make sure that the children were neat and clean for these visits.

Mrs Mann! I say, Mrs Mann, are you in there?

CLANG!
CLANG!

*Parish official

Mr Bumble walked back to the main workhouse with Oliver trotting beside him. The boy asked every quarter of a mile whether they were nearly there. Mr Bumble returned very short and snappish replies to these questions.

Shortly after they reached the workhouse, Mr Bumble informed Oliver that the board had said he was to appear before it immediately.

What is your name, boy?

Answer the gentleman.

Oliver... Oliver Twist.

Hmmm! It's obvious that this boy is a fool.

You know you're an orphan, I suppose? You know you've got no father or mother?

Yes, sir.

I hope you say your prayers every night, and pray for the people who feed you and take care of you.

You have come here to be taught a useful trade. You'll begin to pick oakum* tomorrow morning at six o'clock. Dismissed!

Oliver was hurried away to a large room. There, on a rough, hard bed, he sobbed himself to sleep.

*Tarred fibre used in shipbuilding

Oliver soon got used to his surroundings. When he dined with the other boys, he enjoyed the one ladle of gruel. Like all the other boys, his bowl never needed washing after meals.

Oliver and his companions suffered slow starvation for three months. At last, they got so wild with hunger that a council was held.

Lots were cast to decide who should walk up to the master after supper that evening, and ask for more. This duty fell to Oliver.

What? Why you little--

Sir...

What is it? What do you want?

Please, sir. I want some more.

The notice concerning Oliver stayed up for a week with no enquiries. Finally, the board was approached by a local chimney sweep, Mr Gamfield.

If you would like this boy to learn a trade in a good, respectable chimney sweeping business, I am ready to take him!

Yours is a nasty trade, Mr Gamfield. Young boys have died doing your job. I'm afraid this board cannot approve of this.

So you won't let me have him, gentlemen?

We never said that, Mr Gamfield. But as it's a nasty business, we think you should take something less than the amount we offered.

Oliver Twist was offered to Mr Gamfield for three pounds and ten cents.

Mr Bumble was ordered to bring Oliver to the magistrate's office.

You're going to be made an apprentice, Oliver. The kind gentlemen are going to make a man of you.

Come on, Oliver. And mind your manners!

This is the boy, Your Worship.

Well, I suppose the boy is fond of chimney sweeping?

He dotes on it, Your Worship.

The next morning, the public was once again informed that Oliver Twist was 'To Let'. Five pounds would be paid to anybody who would take him.

A short time after the notice went up, Mr Bumble came across Mr Sowerberry, the mortician*, who agreed to take the boy. Mr Bumble was more than eager to send the boy to his new master as soon as possible.

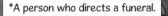

*A person who directs a funeral.

Good evening, Mr Sowerberry.

Ah, Mr Bumble! I see you have brought the boy. Come in, come in, both of you!

Try to be a good boy, Oliver. And for heaven's sake, mind your manners!

My dear, this is the boy from the workhouse I told you about.

He is very young!

Oh yes, he is young, Mrs Sowerberry. There is no denying that, but he'll grow.

Ah! I dare say he will, but on our food and drink!

13

I see no point in saving parish children. You lot always cost more to keep than you're worth.

Get downstairs, you little bag of bones! Charlotte, give this boy some of the cold bits we left out for the dog!

Oliver had a better time at the mortician's than he had had at the workhouse. But it wasn't without troubles. Mrs Sowerberry came to dislike Oliver more and more as the days wore on.

Put your back into your job, Workhouse!

And then there was Noah Claypole, a charity boy*. He had been looked down upon all his life by his betters, and had now found a victim in Oliver.

*A student in a school for the poor and helpless.

Oh, Noah! Why don't you leave Oliver alone and come join me for tea?

But everybody lets him alone enough! Neither his father nor his mother will ever interfere with him! Ha ha ha!

Ha ha ha! Oh, Noah!

And because of her affection for Noah, Charlotte was also beginning to dislike Oliver.

Noah sensed that Oliver was becoming Mr Sowerberry's pet. Feeling his seniority threatened, he made life more difficult for the orphan.

Tell me, Workhouse, how's your mother?

She's dead. And don't you say anything about her to me!

What did she die of, Workhouse?

Of a broken heart, our nurses told me. I think I know what it must be to die of that.

Well, tol de rol lol lol, Workhouse! You must know, your mother was a bad woman.

It's a great deal better, Workhouse, that she died when she did, or else she'd have been serving hard labour in Bridewell Prison, or--

He'll murder me! Charlotte! HELP! HELP!

Blimey! Missus! Missus! Oliver's gone mad!

Noah's shouts were responded to by a loud scream from Charlotte, and a louder one from Mrs Sowerberry, who rushed into the kitchen.

Noah rose from the ground and pommelled the helpless lad until he fell unconscious.

When they could tear and beat no longer, they dragged Oliver, struggling and shouting, into the dust cellar, where they locked him up.

Noah, call Mr. Bumble now!

Oh, Mr Bumble! The boy is mad!

Mr Bumble took himself with all speed to the mortician's shop.

Meat, ma'am, meat. You've overfed him. If you had kept him on gruel, none of this would have happened!

WHAM! THUMP!

What is all this, boy? What brought this on?

Noah called my mother names!

Now, dear, please--

And what if he did, you ungrateful wretch! She probably deserved what he said, and worse!

She didn't!

She did!

That's a lie!

Don't you ever lie about my mother again!

It was the flood of tears that left Mr Sowerberry with no alternative.

Had he hesitated for one instant to punish Oliver most severely, he would have been branded a brute and an insulting creature by Mrs Sowerberry.

WHAP!

Mr Sowerberry gave Oliver a thrashing which satisfied even Mrs Sowerberry, and made Mr Bumble's cane unnecessary.

That night, Mrs Sowerberry, after making further offensive remarks about his mother, ordered Oliver to his dismal bed.

At the first ray of light, Oliver rose, and unbarred the door. With one timid look around, he closed it behind him, and was in the open street.

In the stillness of the gloomy workshop, Oliver finally gave way to his feelings.

Oliver quickly decided that he would make his way to London, which was such a large city that no one, not even Mr Bumble, could ever find him there.

Oliver had to walk over seventy miles with nothing to eat, except what he could beg from strangers.

When he arrived at the town of Barnet, Oliver saw a boy eyeing him most earnestly from the opposite side of the street. After a while, he crossed over.

Hello mate! What's the matter?

I am very hungry and tired, but I must get to London!

Going to London? Got any lodgings or money?

No--

Don't fret! I've got to be in London tonight, and I know a respectable old gentleman there who will give you lodgings for nothing.

This young man was called Jack Dawkins, but he was better known as the Artful Dodger.

They reached a narrow and muddy street in London after nightfall, and entered a house near Field Lane.

This is my friend Oliver Twist, Fagin.

We are very glad to see you, Oliver.

Welcome, Oliver! Nice to meet you.

Let me take your jacket, Oliver!

I'll take your cap for you, Oliver!

Give me that heavy bundle, Oliver!

Off with the lot of you! Dodger, bring the sausages! And fetch a pint for Oliver.

The next morning, Fagin and Oliver were joined by Dodger and Charley Bates, one of the boys Oliver had met the night before.

I hope you've been at work this morning, my dears?

Hard! Two pocketbooks!

Wipes!

Not as heavy as they should be. But nicely made, yes, Oliver?

Indeed, sir!

He is so naïve!

I was only marvelling at your hard work.

Never mind him, Oliver. Stick with me!

Sometime later, two young ladies, Nancy and Bet, called to see the young gentlemen. Oliver liked their pleasant manners very much.

After some days, Oliver obtained the permission he had so eagerly sought. The old man gave his assent, and told Oliver that he could go with the boys to work.

The next morning, the three boys set out. Oliver wondered where they were going, and what kind of work he would be taught first.

Dodger, we have been walking for almost an hour. When do we get to work?

Soon, Charley started stealing from the shops. Oliver was so shocked that he was on the point of seeking his way back, when...

Hush!

What's the matter?

Over there, across the street--

BOOK STALL

See the gentleman by the bookstall, Oliver? He'll do!

The magistrate, Mr Fang, was out of temper when Oliver was brought before him.

Common thievery, Your Worship. The boy stole this gentleman's pocketbook.

Your Honour, if I may--

What is the charge, Officer?

What is your name, sir?

My name, sir, is Brownlow. Allow me to ask--

Hold your tongue, sir, or I'll have you turned out of this office!

Are there any witnesses?

None, Your Worship!

Will you state your complaint against this boy?

Sir, I fear this boy is ill.

Oh, yes, I dare say!

Come, none of your tricks here, you young fellow! What's your name?

I think he really is ill, Your Worship.

Nonsense! I know better.

Oliver fell heavily to the floor in a fainting fit, but no one dared to stir.

Let him lie there; he'll soon be tired of that!

The boy stands sentenced for three months! Hard labour, of course.

Wait!

Wait! Don't take him away! I keep the bookstall, Mr Fang. I saw it all! The robbery was committed by another boy!

Really? Why did you not come sooner then?

I didn't have anybody to mind my shop, Mr Fang! I could not get anybody till five minutes ago, and then I ran here all the way!

The boy is discharged! Clear the office!

Poor boy, poor boy!

Call a coach, somebody... immediately!

Mr Brownlow decided to take the boy to his home near Pentonville. It was not too far from where the boy had first entered London in the company of Dodger.

24

For many days, Oliver remained insensible to the goodness of his new friends.

All the while, he was looked after by his new benefactor and his housekeeper, the sweet and motherly Mrs Bedwin.

In Mrs Bedwin's room, Oliver would stare most intently at a portrait.

Are you fond of pictures, dear?

What a beautiful, mild face that lady has. Who is she?

Why, really, I don't know. It seems to strike your fancy, dear.

She is so very pretty. But the eyes are so sorrowful. It looks as if the picture is alive, and wants to speak to me...

Poor boy, poor boy!

Have you given him any food, Bedwin?

He has just had a bowl of nourishing broth, sir.

Ugh! A couple of glasses of port wine would have done him much more good.

The idea of resemblance between Oliver's features and some familiar face came upon Mr Brownlow so strongly that he could not withdraw his gaze.

Why! What is this?! Mrs Bedwin! Look here!

As he spoke, Mr Brownlow pointed hastily to the picture on the wall near Oliver, and then to the boy's face, which was the portrait's living copy.

Oliver could not know the cause of this sudden exclamation, for, not being strong enough to bear the shock it gave him, he fainted.

Mr Brownlow and Mrs Bedwin weren't the only people concerned about Oliver. There were others, like the young criminals who were responsible for Oliver's near brush with the law.

Rest, my boy, rest.

Where's Oliver? Where's the boy, Dodger? Speak out or I'll strangle you!

The police caught him, and that's all about it.

You dirty--

Why, what the--!

Oh, Heavens!

SPLASH!

Nobody but an infernal, rich, plundering old thief could afford to throw away any drink but water!

You're ill-treating your boys again? Why they don't just get up and murder you is beyond me!

Who pitched that beer at me?

Hush! Hush! You seem out of humour, Bill Sikes...

Please, Bill, sit down. You too, Nancy. Something has come up that we must discuss.

After pacifying his friend with three glasses of beer, Fagin began to tell Bill Sikes all about Oliver Twist...

...and how the boy might spell trouble for them all.

That's very likely! Fagin, you've blown it!

Somebody must find out what's been done at the police station!

Yes, Nancy can do that.

I'm afraid that if the game is up for us, it might be up for a good many more!

Me? No, Fagin! Don't even start that!

You're just the right person for this, Nancy! Nobody here knows anything about you, especially the police.

And I don't want them to either! I won't go, Bill!

She'll go, Fagin.

No I won'- -ugh!

Yes, she will, Fagin!

And so Nancy was sent off to the police station, dressed in more suitable clothing taken from Fagin's inexhaustible stock.

At the police station, Nancy posed as Oliver's deeply affected sister. The policeman who had arrested Oliver informed her that the boy had been taken ill, and discharged...

Nancy returned by the most complicated route she could think of to Fagin's house.

No sooner Sikes heard the account than he hastily departed.

....and that the prosecutor had carried him away to his own home, near Pentonville.

We must know where he is, my dears! Oliver must be found! Charley, lurk about until you bring home some news of him.

I shall shut this shop tonight. You'll know where to find me.

The world of filth that Fagin and his companions inhabited was far removed from the world that Mr Brownlow had opened up to Oliver.

Two weeks later, there came a chance visit from an old acquaintance of Mr Brownlow.

Pardon me, Mr Brownlow. Mr Grimwig has come calling.

Is he coming up?

Yes, sir.

That's the boy, is it? How are you, boy?

Much better, thank you, sir.

Mr Brownlow, realising that his friend was about to say something displeasing, asked Oliver to step downstairs.

Oliver, Mr Grimwig is a very old and dear friend of mine.

I'll eat my head, sir! Who's that?

This is young Oliver Twist, whom we were talking about.

He is a nice-looking boy, is he not?

Where does he come from? Who is he? He has had a fever. What of that? Fevers are not peculiar to good people, are they?

Mr Grimwig was strongly tempted to admit that Oliver's appearance and manners were unusually appealing. But he liked to contradict whatever he heard.

And when are you going to hear a full account of the life and adventures of Oliver Twist?

Tomorrow morning. I would rather he was alone with me at the time.

Tomorrow? He is deceiving you, my good friend!

Excuse me, Mr Brownlow. I hope I'm not disturbing you.

A boy came around with the books you ordered, sir.

Stop the boy, Mrs Bedwin. There is something that needs to go back with him.

He has gone, sir.

Dear me, I am sorry for that. I particularly wished some books to be returned tonight.

Send Oliver with them. He will be sure to deliver them safely.

Yes, do let me take them, if you please, sir! I'll run all the way, sir!

Mr Brownlow sent Oliver off to return the books to the bookseller and pay his bill with a five-pound note. He asked Oliver to return quickly with the change.

Oliver made his way down the street and away from Mr Brownlow's house. Mr Brownlow watched him, certain that Oliver would return soon.

Meanwhile, in the obscure parlour of a low tavern, situated in the filthiest part of Little Saffron Hill, Bill Sikes and Fagin sat brooding.

Well, well, my dear, I know all that; we have a mutual interest, Bill.

No more excuses, Fagin. Find the boy! If I go, you go! So take care of me!

You are on the scent, are you, Nancy?

Yes, I am, Bill. The brat's been ill--

Nancy suddenly checked herself, and turned the conversation to other matters.

Meanwhile, Oliver, little dreaming that he was within such a short distance of Fagin, accidentally turned down a bylane.

He was walking along, thinking how happy and contented he ought to feel, when...

31

No, I haven't! Don't even think that, Fagin!

Keep quiet, will you?

No, I won't do that either!

Fagin felt it would be unsafe to prolong any conversation with Nancy. He turned to Oliver.

So you wanted to get away, my dear? Wanted to call for the police, did you?

Well, we'll cure you of that, my young master!

What do you mean by this? Do you know who you are and what you are?

I won't stand by and see it done, Fagin! You've got the boy. Let him be!

I wish I had been struck dead before I had lent a hand in bringing this boy here!

Fagin, I thieved for you when I was a child, not half as old as this boy! I have been in the same trade, and in the same service, for twelve years! Don't you know that?

Nancy made a few ineffectual struggles against Sikes, and then fainted.

Ohhhhhh...

Some days after Oliver fell back into the clutches of Fagin and his gang, Mr Bumble was in London on business when he happened to spy an advertisement that caught his attention.

'FIVE GUINEAS REWARD, A young boy, named Oliver Twist, absconded, or was abducted, last Thursday evening from his home at Pentonville. The above reward will be paid to any person who will give information that will lead to the discovery of Oliver Twist or throw any light upon his history, in which the for many reasons, interested.'

Mr Bumble, in something more than five minutes, was on his way to Pentonville.

You don't happen to know anything good about him, do you, Mr Bumble?

I'm afraid not, sir.

Then I fear it is all true.

This is not much for your information, but I would gladly have given you triple this amount if it had been favourable to the boy.

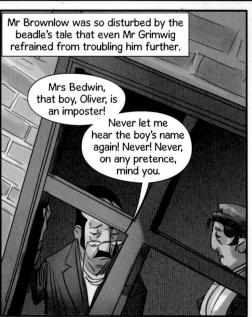

Mr Brownlow was so disturbed by the beadle's tale that even Mr Grimwig refrained from troubling him further.

Mrs Bedwin, that boy, Oliver, is an imposter!

Never let me hear the boy's name again! Never! Never, on any pretence, mind you.

About noon the next day, Fagin took the opportunity of lecturing Oliver on the sin of ingratitude, of which he had been guilty.

Later that evening, Fagin went to visit Bill Sikes to discuss how Oliver could start to earn his keep in the gang.

There they began to discuss a robbery at Chertsey that they had been planning.

What if the job could be done safely from the outside? Would that be worth something extra to you?

Yes.

The place is barred up at night like a jail, but there is one part we can crack easily.

But we'll need a small boy to pull this off.

I have someone in mind.

Who?

Not in front of Nancy.

Nancy, love! Fetch us another jug of beer!

You don't want any beer.

Now, Fagin! You can tell Bill about Oliver!

Ha! You're a clever one, my dear; the sharpest girl I ever saw!

The girl held Oliver fast by the hand and continued to pour the warnings and assurances she had already given, into his ear.

Oliver glanced hurriedly at the empty street, and a cry for help hung upon his lips. But Nancy's voice was in his ear, and he didn't have the heart to utter it.

Oliver hesitated to yell out, and the opportunity was gone. All too soon, he was in the house, and the door was shut.

I'm glad to hear it. Come here, boy, and let me read you a lecture, and get it done.

So you've got the kid. Did he come quietly?

Like a lamb.

Now first, do you know what this is?

Yes...

I want you to know this is always loaded.

If you speak a word when you're outdoors with me, except when I speak to you, this bullet will be in your head without notice.

So, if you do decide to speak without permission, say your prayers first.

39

It was a cheerless morning when they got into the street. Sikes gave very little attention to the numerous sights and sounds which astonished the boy so much.

They made their way through Hosier Lane into Holborn.

Along the way, Sikes stopped a cart and asked the driver if he would give them a lift to Isleworth. Much to Oliver's relief, the driver agreed.

After a time, they came to a public house where the cart stopped.

Sikes and Oliver lingered at the public house for a while. Then they got a ride with another driver to Shepperton. As they passed the Sunbury Church, the clock struck seven.

Coach and Horses

Sikes dismounted, and rapped his side-pocket in a very significant manner.

The cart stopped after two or three miles. They walked on, but turned into no house. They kept walking in the mud and darkness, until they came within sight of the lights of a nearby town.

The trio arrived at Chertsey, and hurried through the town, which was deserted at such a late hour.

After walking about for a quarter of a mile, they stopped.

The boy next! Hoist him up, and I'll catch him.

For the first time, Oliver was mad with grief and terror when he saw that housebreaking and robbery, if not murder, were the objects of the outing.

Keep going, boy! Do it, or I'll blow your brains out now!

Here, Bill! I have managed to pull the shutter open. Once the boy is inside, he'll be ready to do his part, I hope.

Listen, boy! You go through there!

Take this light and go softly up the steps straight before you, and along the little hall, to the street door. Unfasten it, and let us in.

See the stairs, boy?

Yes...

It'll be done in a minute, boy! Do your work!

Bill, you hear something?

It's nothing, Toby. **Now!**

Oliver firmly resolved that he would make one effort to dart upstairs from the hall, and alarm the family.

Ugh!

BLAM!

Suddenly, the door before Oliver flew open. Scared by the sudden breaking of the dead stillness of the place, Oliver let his lantern fall.

Clasp your arm tighter!

They've hit him! Quick! How the boy bleeds! Let us first tie a bandage on his wound.

KA-RAZ!

Sikes and Toby dragged Oliver for several yards, but there came the loud ringing of a bell, mingled with the noise of firearms and the shouts of men. The two criminals panicked.

Forget the boy! He's as good as dead! Come on!

43

Bill Sikes and Toby Crackit ran off as a party from the house searched the grounds for the intruders. Because of the cold, the search did not last long, and the party did not find Oliver.

The air grew colder as the morning wore on.

Oh... ugh...

Trembling in every joint from cold and exhaustion, Oliver made an effort to stand erect. A creeping sickness seemed to warn him that if he lay there, he would surely die.

In the meantime, Mr Giles, the household butler, and Brittles, a handyman, were in the kitchen recounting the events of that morning. They were the men who had discovered the break-in.

It was half past two when I heard the noise! A bursting noise--

Like that, Mr Giles?

KNOCK

KNOCK

The rogues have returned! Come, Brittles! We must investigate!

44

About an hour later, Mr Losberne, the local doctor, arrived at the house. He found Rose and her aunt, Mrs Maylie, tending to Oliver as best as they could.

This is a curious case.

The doctor was with Oliver much longer than either he or the ladies had expected. The bedroom bell was rung very often, and the servants ran up and down the stairs all the time.

Sometime later, the doctor returned, looking very sombre.

Mr Losberne, he's not in danger, I hope?

I don't think he is. He's perfectly quiet and comfortable now. You can meet him.

Stepping into the room, instead of the dogged ruffian they had expected to see, they saw a mere child, worn out with pain and exhaustion, and sunk into a deep sleep.

Oh, my... I... I'm so happy...

The boy will wake up in an hour or two, Mrs Maylie. Then, I think, we can speak to him without danger.

It was late evening before the kindhearted doctor brought them the news that the boy was well enough to talk.

The meeting was a long one, for Oliver told them all his whole history. The boy was often compelled to stop because of pain and lack of strength.

Oliver's mind was so troubled with anxiety to disclose something that the doctor thought it better to give him some time to talk about it.

It was a solemn thing to hear, the feeble voice of the sick child recounting the details of the troubles that hard, evil men had brought upon him.

Immediately after the important interview, Oliver needed to rest again. The doctor, after wiping his eyes, agreed with Mrs Maylie that Oliver would be better off with her and Rose.

Oliver's hair was smoothed by Rose's gentle hands that night. She watched him as he slept. He felt calm and happy, and could have died without a murmur.

As the days passed, Oliver gradually recovered under the care of Mrs Maylie, Rose, and the kindhearted Mr Losberne.

In addition to the pain of a bullet injury, Oliver's exposure to the wet and cold had brought on a fever. He was sick for many weeks, but gradually, began to get better.

I hope I can do something to show my gratitude to you and your aunt.

Poor fellow! You will have many opportunities to serve us. We are going into the country, and my aunt intends to take you with us.

Ma'am, how kind of you!

But I must see the kindly old gentleman and the nurse who took care of me. If they knew how happy I am, they would be pleased, I am sure.

I am sure they would. And Mr Losberne has already been kind enough to promise that, when you are well enough, he will take you to see them.

In a short time, Oliver recovered enough to make this journey.

As Oliver knew the name of the street on which Mr Brownlow lived, they could drive straight to it. When the carriage turned into it, the boy's heart beat violently.

Now, my boy, which house is it?

The white house! Oh, hurry up!

You will see them right away, and they will be overjoyed to find you safe and well.

Oh dear...

A servant next door told Oliver that Mr Brownlow had sold off his goods, and gone to the West Indies six weeks earlier.

Alas! The white house was empty.

Has his housekeeper gone too?

Yes, sir. The old gentleman, the housekeeper, and a friend of Mr Brownlow's.

Knock at the next door. Perhaps they know what has become of Mr Brownlow.

Bitter with disappointment, Mr Losberne and Oliver left London and returned to Mrs Maylie's.

TOLET

Oliver was upset, and his friends got ready to take him to the country.

In a fortnight, the weather was fine and warm, and Oliver and his friends left the house at Chertsey to go to the country.

Giles and another servant were left to care for the house.

Who can describe the pleasure and delight the sickly boy felt! He was in the balmy air and among the green hills and rich woods of an inland village.

It was a lovely place to which they retired. Oliver seemed to come into a new existence there.

It was a happy time.

Oliver walked with Mrs Maylie and Rose, listening to them talk about books. Sometimes, he sat near them, in some shady place, and listened as the young lady read.

Oliver was happy if they wanted a flower that he could climb to reach, or if he could run to bring something they had forgotten at home.

Three months glided away. One night, Rose sat down at the piano as usual.

SOB SOB

She tried to play some lively tune, but was unable to supress her tears. Soon she took to bed, and in a short time, grew deadly pale.

I hope nothing is the matter. She didn't look well tonight.
I hope not, Oliver. I have been very happy with her for some years. Too happy perhaps. It may be time that I meet with some misfortune...
...but I hope it is not this. The heavy blow of losing the dear girl who has so long been my comfort and happiness!
But she was quite well a couple of hours ago.
She is very ill now, and will be worse. My dear, dear, Rose! Oh, what will I do without her!
Consider, ma'am, how young and good she is, and what pleasure and comfort she gives to everyone around her.
She will not die! Heaven will never let her die so young!
You think like a child, Oliver. But you teach me my duty. It is not always the youngest and best who are spared for those who love them. But Heaven is just.

When morning came, Rose was at the first stage of a high and dangerous fever.

Oliver, this letter must be sent as soon as possible to Mr Losberne. He needs to be here.

Now be on your way, Oliver! And please, dear, hurry!

Here is another letter, but I am not sure whether to send it now, or wait until I see how Rose gets on. I would not forward it unless I feared the worst.

Will it go, ma'am?

I think not. I will wait until tomorrow.

Oliver ran quickly across the fields and down little lanes, and stopped now and then only to catch his breath.

At last, he came to the little marketplace of the town.

Once in the town, Oliver rushed to The George, where he was taken to the landlord.

So, Mr Losberne in Chertsey? No worries, young master! I'll see this is sent out right away!

THE GEORGE INN

Oliver was ready to run back to Mrs Maylie with a much lighter heart. He turned around and....

THUMP!

I beg your pardon, sir!

What the devil's this?

I was in a great hurry to get home. I didn't see you coming!

I am sorry! I hope I have not hurt you.

Curses on your head and black death on your heart, you imp! What are you doing here?

The stranger loomed threateningly over Oliver, as if intending to strike a blow at him, but fell violently on the ground, writhing and foaming in a fit.

After he was carried into the hotel, Oliver turned towards home, running as fast as he could, to make up for lost time.

Rose had rapidly grown worse, and, before midnight, was delirious. The local doctor constantly attended to her.

The girl's illness is most alarming, Mrs Maylie. It would be little short of a miracle if she recovered.

Not even the arrival of Mr Losberne gave the household much hope. Rose had fallen into a deep sleep. She would wake up from it, either to recover or to bid them farewell and die.

Oliver crept to the old churchyard and prayed for Rose.

One day, as the sun began to set, Mr Losberne entered the parlour.

What about Rose? Tell me at once. I can't bear it. My dear child! She is dying!

No! As God is good and merciful, she will live to bless us all for years to come!

It was too much happiness to bear.

Oliver felt stunned and dazed by the unexpected news. He could not weep, or speak, or rest.

I thank you, my boy, for giving me such wonderful news! And you are--?

This is Oliver Twist, Mr Harry. This is the young lad your mother and Miss Rose have taken under their wings.

I'm Harry, Mrs Maylie's son, Oliver.

Giles, I think you had better go on to my mother's in the coach. I would rather walk, so that I have a little time before I see her. You can say I am coming.

I beg your pardon, Mr Harry, but if you would let coach boy say that, I will be obliged. The journey has left me tired and dishevelled, and if the maids see me in this state, I'll never have authority over them again!

You can do as you like, Giles.

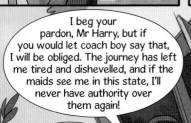

The coach boy headed off, and Giles, Mr Maylie, and Oliver followed at their leisure.

The inmates of the house rushed out to search for Fagin.

But the search was in vain. There were no traces of recent footprints. They decided that no one could have gained so much ground in such a short time.

It must have been a dream, Oliver.

Fagin... Fagin was here!

Who was the other?

Oh no, sir! I saw him too clearly for that! I saw them both, as clearly as I see you now!

The very same man who came so suddenly upon me at the inn!

The two gentlemen watched Oliver's earnest face. They seemed satisfied about the accuracy of what he said.

The grass was long, but it was not trodden down except for where their feet had crushed it. Still, the men did not give up until nightfall when searching further seemed hopeless. So, they gave up the search with some reluctance.

After a few days, the affair was forgotten. Meanwhile, Rose had left her room and was able to go out again. Yet, there was tension in the cottage.

More than once, Rose appeared with traces of tears upon her face.

One morning, when Rose was alone in the breakfast parlour...

May I speak to you for a few moments, Rose?

I ought to have left earlier--

You should have. Forgive me, but I wish you had.

I came here only because I feared that you were dying. I thought I was losing you.

You really did not want me to be here with you?

I did not mean that. I only wish you had left, so that you could have turned to high and noble pursuits again – to pursuits worthy of you.

There is no pursuit worthier than you, Rose.

For years, I have loved you. Now, I give you the heart that has been yours for so long. Dear Rose, please, I beg you, marry--

Harry, you must forget me! Never as your friend, but as the object of your love!

I am a friendless girl with a blot on her name! Marrying me would only hinder your progress in the world. I can't hold you back, Harry...

Rose, please!

If I had been less fortunate... if I had been poor, sick, helpless, would you have turned from me then?

Do not press me to reply. That question does not arise, and never will!

It is unfair, unkind, to urge it!

Harry was visibly upset and decided to leave. As Mr Losberne was eager to be his travelling companion, the two got ready to leave the next morning.

Everyone came out to see the men off, with one notable exception.

He seems in high spirits and happy. I am glad!

Drive on. Hard, fast, full gallop! Nothing short of flying will keep pace with me today!

But the tears which ran down Rose's face, seemed to tell more of sorrow than joy.

One summer evening, not long after Harry and Mr Losberne's departure, a most sinister meeting took place in London. The first party of this meeting was Mr Bumble and his new bride.

Mr Bumble had been made the master of the workhouse. He had married Mrs Corney, the matron of the workhouse. Together, the couple enjoyed a reign of terror.

The place should be somewhere here.

Mind what I told you, otherwise you'll betray us at once!

Hello, there! Stand still a minute. I'll be with you right away.

Come in! Don't keep me waiting now!

The woman walked boldly in. Mr Bumble followed.

What the devil made you linger in the rain?

Come with me! We've business to do!

We... we were only cooling ourselves, Monks!

Monks led the Bumbles up the ladder to the second floor of the old building.

So you told your woman why I asked you here?

Indeed! The first question is: what is the worth of my services to you?

Would twenty pounds be enough?

Add five pounds to the sum you have named, and I'll tell you all I know.

Now, Mrs Bumble, tell me about Old Sally, and Oliver Twist's mother.

Old Sally was the nurse who helped Oliver's mother in his birth. She was with her when she died. She stole something from the dead woman.

And...

When Sally died, she and I were alone. Just before her death, she spoke to me about Oliver and his mother, and what she had stolen from her.

What did she steal?

That is all. Is that what you expected from me?

A ring and a locket. The ring has 'Agnes' engraved on the inside with a space left blank for a surname. Oh, and it has a date: a year before the boy was born!

It is.

Now, get up and step away from the table, both of you!

65

When they stepped away from the table, Monks suddenly threw open a large trapdoor.

Be calm, both of you. I could have opened this when you were seated over it, were that my game!

If you flung a man's body down there, where would it be tomorrow morning?

Twelve miles down the river, and cut to pieces!

Even if the sea ever gives up its dead, it will keep its silver and gold to itself!

Now get away from here as fast as you can!

And mind you, keep a quiet tongue about this meeting!

Quickly, she tore off her bonnet and cloak and hid them.

Nancy was in no way interested in the arrival of this stranger, until she heard the murmur of the man's voice and recognised it.

Fagin made an excuse and told Nancy to wait for him while he took care of important business.

Any news of the boy?

Yes--

Nancy listened in horror for some time. As the men finished their discussion, Nancy glided back to the room and waited for Fagin to return.

Why, Nancy, how pale you are! What have you been doing?

I've been sitting here for I don't know how long. Come, let me get back before Bill grows any angrier.

When Nancy got into the open street, she was bewildered and unable to think clearly for some time. She then started off in the opposite direction of Sikes's lodging.

Nancy waited for Fagin and the visitor to get settled, and then followed after them.

As the girl made her way down the street, she fought back her tears as she resolved upon something.

Based on the conversation she had overheard, Nancy raced to a hotel off Hyde Park, and there she requested to see a guest, Rose Maylie.

Nancy told Rose everything – about Fagin, the gang of thieves, and her role in Oliver being captured again.

Miss, do you know a man named Monks?

I have never heard that name. Who is he?

He knows you, and knew you were here.

He struck a bargain with Fagin that Oliver should be made a thief. I overheard them speaking the night Monks saw my shadow on the wall of Fagin's parlour... and I overheard them tonight again.

If you repeat this information to my friend in the next room, he can take you to a place of safety without delay.

It is too late for me, miss. Amongst them is one I can't leave.

Monks also bought and destroyed what little evidence there was to prove Oliver's lineage. And thus, he destroyed whatever could prove that he is Oliver's brother!

His brother!

Where can I find you again?

Every Sunday night, from eleven until the clock strikes twelve, I will walk on London Bridge – if I am alive.

And with that, Nancy left.

The news about Oliver's brother weighed heavily on Rose's mind. As she was wondering what to do, Oliver came to her with great news.

Eager to help Oliver, and to seek help regarding Monks, Rose arranged to go and see the old gentleman the next day.

Mr Brownlow, you once showed great kindness to a young friend of mine. I am sure you will take an interest in hearing of him again. His name is Oliver Twist.

I found Mr Brownlow! I saw him getting out of a coach and entering a house. I could not dare to speak to him, but Giles confirmed that it was his house.

At Mr Brownlow's urging, Rose revealed that Oliver was waiting downstairs. The reunion between the old gentleman and Oliver was most touching, overshadowed only by the lad's reunion with Mrs Bedwin.

My innocent boy!

Young lady, if you have any evidence that will change my unfavourable opinion of that child, please give it to me.

Rose related all that had happened to Oliver since he left Mr Brownlow's house, holding back Nancy's information. She said that Oliver's only sorrow had been not being able to meet his old friend.

Mr Brownlow, there is something I need to discuss with you about Oliver. It has to do with a man named Monks...

In hushed tones, Rose revealed everything Nancy had told her.

The next morning, Rose cautiously informed Mrs Maylie and Mr Losberne about everything she had learnt. A little later, they assembled at Mr Brownlow's residence where Mr Grimwig was already present.

We must discover Oliver's parentage. We must regain his inheritance for him. He has been deprived of it by fraud.

How can we do this?

Leave that task to me. Rose and I will go and see Nancy next Sunday night.

I suggest we bring one other person into our confidence – Miss Rose's very old friend, Harry Maylie.

It is quite clear that we must bring this man, Monks, to his knees. To do that, we must catch him when he is not surrounded by these people.

Harry was acc added to the

Fagin's den of thieves had suffered a great loss earlier that morning. Dodger had been arrested for stealing a snuffbox. But that wasn't troubling Fagin's mind.

Have you noticed anything queer about Nancy of late, Charley?

She seems distant, distracted.

Ha ha ha! If I had to put up with Sikes like she has to, I'd have more worries than I could handle!

Charley, the new boy, he knows Nancy?

Bring the new boy here, Charley. I have a job for him...

Next Sunday, Nancy walked on London Bridge as she had promised. As Rose and Mr Losberne approached her, the trio was unaware that they were being observed by one of Fagin's boys.

Nancy, we--

Not here. I am afraid to speak to you here. Come away, out of the public road, down the steps over there.

I don't know why, but I feel such fear and dread tonight that I can hardly stand. Horrible thoughts of death make me burn as if I were on fire.

72

It's only your imagination, girl. I've often had feelings like this myself.

No imagination! This is all too real.

Speak to her kindly. Poor creature! She seems to need it!

Listen, Nancy. We propose to force the secret from Monks.

But if Monks refuses to cooperate with us, you must give up Fagin.

I will not do it! Devil that he is, I will never do that!

Fagin and I have lived bad lives! Our kind doesn't turn on its own. Just as others did not turn on me when they could have, I can't turn on them!

Then put Monks in my hands. Leave him to me to deal with. You have my word – he will never know who gave him up.

I... I will take your words.

He has a red mark, like a burn or scald on his neck, you say?

I think I may.

You know him?

As Fagin's spy listened, Nancy told Rose and Mr Brownlow that Monks could usually be found at a public house called The Three Cripples.

73

As Rose and Mr Brownlow turned to leave, the astonished listener, making sure that he was alone again, darted away with utmost speed to Fagin's house.

Fagin was humiliated at the thought that his grand scheme for Oliver had come undone. His blood boiled with hatred for Nancy for daring to conspire with strangers against her own kind.

At last! At last!

Just then, Sikes walked in.

There! Take care of this, and do the most you can with it.

What is it, Fagin? Cat got your tongue?

It's rare for you to be at a loss for words. What now? What do you look at me so for?

I've got something to tell you, Bill. And it will make you feel worse than I do.

Tell me, what if one of the lads were to go and blow upon all of us?

Why, I'd grind his skull under the heel of my boot into as many grains as there are hairs upon his head.

What if I did such a thing, Bill? Me, who knows so much, and who could hang so many?

Hours after Sikes went on the run, and the news of the murder spread, Mr Brownlow dispersed several men to The Three Cripples with a full description of Monks. They were told to stay there until he showed up.

How dare you do this to me? This is petty treatment from my father's oldest friend!

It is because I was your father's oldest friend that I am treating you so gently, Edward Leeford!

By whose authority am I kidnapped in the street and brought here by these dogs?

By mine.

What do you want with me?

You have a brother.

I have no brother!

That marriage caused your father nothing but anguish. He was miserable the whole time he was with your mother.

He was relieved when she finally left and took you with her after ten long years.

I know of the wretched marriage into which family pride forced your unhappy father...

...And I know you were the sole and most unnatural product.

When they had been separated for some time, your father fell amongst new friends: a naval officer and his two children.

They were both daughters – a beautiful girl of nineteen, and a child two or three years old.

What is this to me?

They lived in a part of the country where your father had retired. Oh, how that young girl and your father came to love each other!

They were engaged by the end of the year. But then your father had to go to Rome to settle an inheritance. He died there, Edward. I know that, and so do you.

When your mother heard about his fortune, she dragged you to Rome. When your father died, people thought he had left no will, so the whole property fell to her and you.

Before he went abroad, he came to me and entrusted me with this picture – a portrait he had painted himself.

When Oliver was first rescued from Fagin, it was by me! Yes, by me. It was then that his strong resemblance to this picture astonished me.

When I lost the boy, knowing your mother was dead, I came looking for you.

77

You fancy a resemblance between this boy and a dead woman, and declare him my brother? You don't even know if a child was born of this woman!

Within the last fortnight, I've learnt all. You have a brother, and you know him.

There was a will your mother destroyed that mentioned Oliver. There existed proofs of his birth and parentage. Those proofs were destroyed by you.

No! No! No! No!

Because of your deeds, a murder has been done. Will you disclose all?

Yes, I will! I will!

Meanwhile, all of London was looking for Sikes. That made things too hot for the other criminals.

So you and Charley were the only ones who got out when the policemen arrived to arrest Fagin?

Yes.

Looks like trouble has found us!

No! He can't be coming here! I hope not!

The dog's arrival meant his master could not be far behind.

But Bill Sikes was a mere shadow of the man who had terrified and bullied them all for years.

Sikes did not say a word as he entered the room.

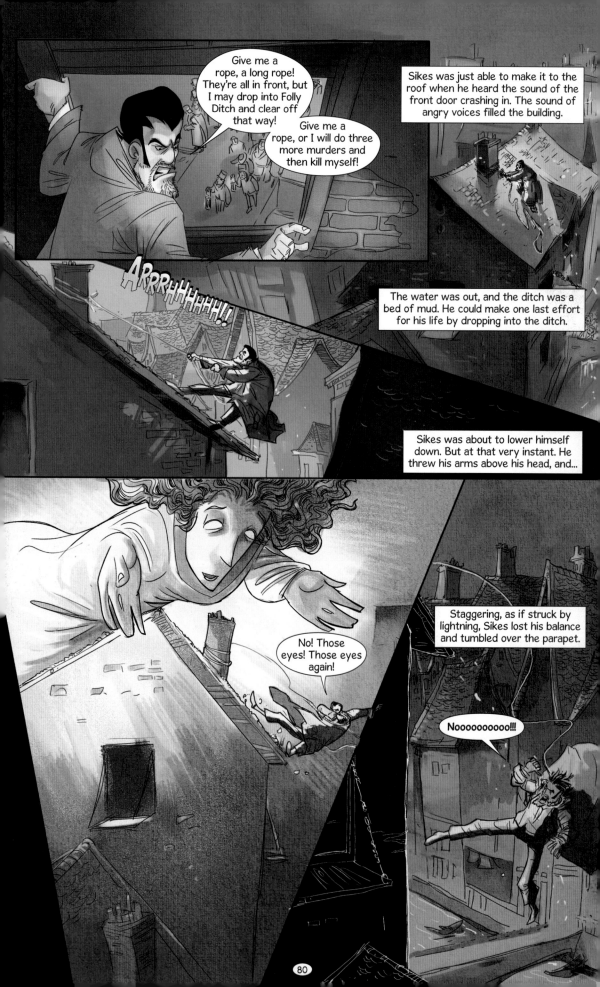

The noose was at his neck. It ran up with his weight, tight as a bowstring and quick as the arrow it speeds. Sikes fell thirty-five feet. There was a sudden jerk, a terrific convulsion of the limbs, and there he hung.

Two days after Sikes's death, Oliver, Rose, Mrs Maylie, and Harry met Mr Brownlow at his request.

Oliver and Rose, who were unaware of the latest developments, felt nervous and uncomfortable.

This is a painful task, but these declarations, which have been signed in London by Monks, must be repeated here.

This child is your half-brother – the illegitimate son of your father, Edwin Leeford, by young Agnes Fleming, who died in giving birth.

Yes...

Oliver listened carefully as Mr Brownlow recounted the story of his father and mother and their ill-fated romance.

Your father had left a letter for your mother, apologising to her for leaving her alone. His will, too, was clear. He divided the bulk of his property into two equal portions – one for Agnes Fleming, and the other for their child.

If the child were a boy, he would inherit his money only so long as he had not stained his name by any public act of dishonour.

That is why Monks wanted to push Oliver into a life of crime!

Mother burnt the will, but she kept the letter and other proof.

Agnes had left her home in secret, and her father died of a broken heart, convinced that his daughter had destroyed herself.

When Mother died, she left her secrets to me.

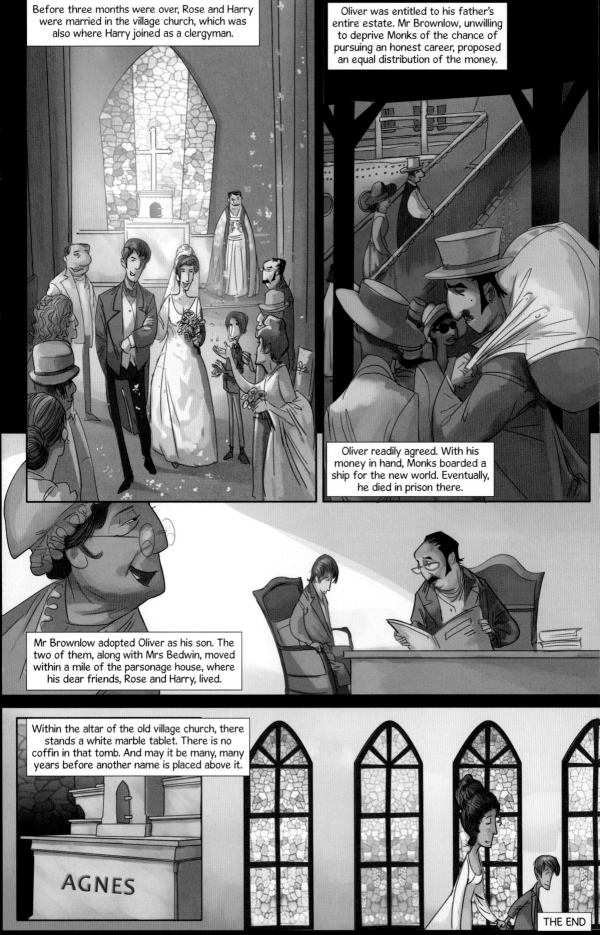

Before three months were over, Rose and Harry were married in the village church, which was also where Harry joined as a clergyman.

Oliver was entitled to his father's entire estate. Mr Brownlow, unwilling to deprive Monks of the chance of pursuing an honest career, proposed an equal distribution of the money.

Oliver readily agreed. With his money in hand, Monks boarded a ship for the new world. Eventually, he died in prison there.

Mr Brownlow adopted Oliver as his son. The two of them, along with Mrs Bedwin, moved within a mile of the parsonage house, where his dear friends, Rose and Harry, lived.

Within the altar of the old village church, there stands a white marble tablet. There is no coffin in that tomb. And may it be many, many years before another name is placed above it.

AGNES

THE END

A delightful tale of adventure set in the pristine, picturesque English countryside.

Adapted by:
Arjun Gaind

Illustrated by:
Sankha Banerjee

No sight makes a man tremble more than seeing Mr Toad behind the wheel of a car…

On a fine summer day, Mole is busy spring cleaning his underground home. When he decides he's had enough of cleaning, Mole ventures towards a place he has never seen before – the river. There he meets Ratty, who takes Mole for a ride in his rowing boat. The two of them become close friends, and spend their time enjoying lazy days by the river. But then they make the mistake of visiting Mr Toad.

Toad is rich, exuberant, but also reckless. When he purchases his very first automobile, Toad, Ratty, and Mole are plunged into a dangerous adventure involving theft, a prison break, and the famous siege of Toad Hall.

Since its first publication in 1908, Kenneth Grahame's story has amused millions of readers, both children and adults. Now with cutting edge visuals and a faithful conversion to a new format, Campfire brings you the definitive version of an all-time classic.

Bringing Dickens's times to life

The London of Dickens's imagination is essentially the London of the 1820s. However, the London that he wrote about was very different from what it is now. Although Dickens exaggerated quite often to drive his point home, given below are glimpses of the conditions of those times, and they are NOT exaggerated!

- The streets were extremely filthy. Each major crossing had a street sweeper who, for a penny, would sweep the street before one crossed it. This was the only way to save one's shoes from getting soiled!

- People belonging to the middle class washed only their hands, neck, and arms regularly, and the poor barely bathed at all!

- In 1834, the British government passed the Poor Law Amendment Act. According to this act, the poor could receive food and shelter only if they adhered to the strict rules of a workhouse, a shelter for homeless people. These workhouses were deliberately made to be horrible places to discourage the poor from viewing them as alternatives to living on the streets. The quantity of food was meagre, no personal possessions were allowed, and children were regularly separated from their parents.

- The elegance of Regent Street, built while Dickens was young, testified to the wealth of London. This street was one of the thoroughfares separating fashionable London from its poor and dirty suburbs.

Dickens's novels reflected the social conditions of his days in minute detail. They were published in monthly or weekly instalments, and were eagerly awaited. The effect of his writing was sensational. When Dickens killed the character of Little Nell in *The Old Curiosity Shop*, the Irish nationalist legislator, Daniel O'Connel, while travelling in a train, flung his copy out of the window crying, 'He should not have killed her,' before breaking down and sobbing!

If we lived in Victorian England, this is how we would have spoken:

'What is your monekeer (name)?'

'Will you have a shat o' gatter (pot of beer) after all this dowry of parny (lot of rain)?'

'Anointed' meant 'knowing' or 'ripe for mischief'. Now you know why kings were anointed – they were ready for mischief!

'If you want a healthy box of ivory (teeth), you better brush twice a day!'

'Fives' meant the fingers. Now you know where the term 'give me five!' comes from!

WHY THAT GRIM POSE?

Ever wondered why the people in all the portrait photographs taken in the early 19th century sport such a serious look? Well, it was because photographic equipments took a long time to capture an image. Smiles are spontaneous and harder to hold naturally for that long a time, and that explains the grim look in all the photographs taken during that era.

DID YOU KNOW?

In 1864, Charles Fetcher, a French actor, had gifted a miniature Swiss chalet (a type of building made of wood) to Dickens. It arrived at the railway station in fifty-eight separate boxes! Dickens loved it and chose to spend many months writing in the chalet. The chalet could be accessed only through a special tunnel that linked it to Dickens's house, Gad's Hill, in Kent.